THE MYSTERIOUS HUBBUB

Amanda Walsh

Houghton Mifflin Company

Boston 1990

ur ship was sailing to a distant land. The sea was calm and the weather fine.

Suddenly, we heard voices in the air, some of men, some of women. We cupped our hands about our ears, trying to make out the words.

There were other sounds too, weird and terrible and growing louder.

'Man the guns!' shouted the first-mate. 'It's an ambush.'

'No, no, don't be afraid,' said the captain, a knowledgeable man who had been a sailor for many years. 'We are approaching the edge of the Frozen Sea. Last winter, a fierce battle was fought here.'

The captain went on to tell us about this battle.
What we were hearing were the shouts and cries
of men, the sobs and screams of women, the
slashing and clashing of swords and battle-axes,
the shocking and knocking of harnesses and
armour, the neighing and slaying of war-horses.
All the horrible sounds of war had become frozen
in the air.

EEEEAAWW WW

GRUMPHGING

But how was it, I wanted to know, that we were able to hear the din of a battle fought last winter?

'Spring has brought fine weather,' answered the captain. 'The warmth is melting the frozen sounds and releasing them into the air.'

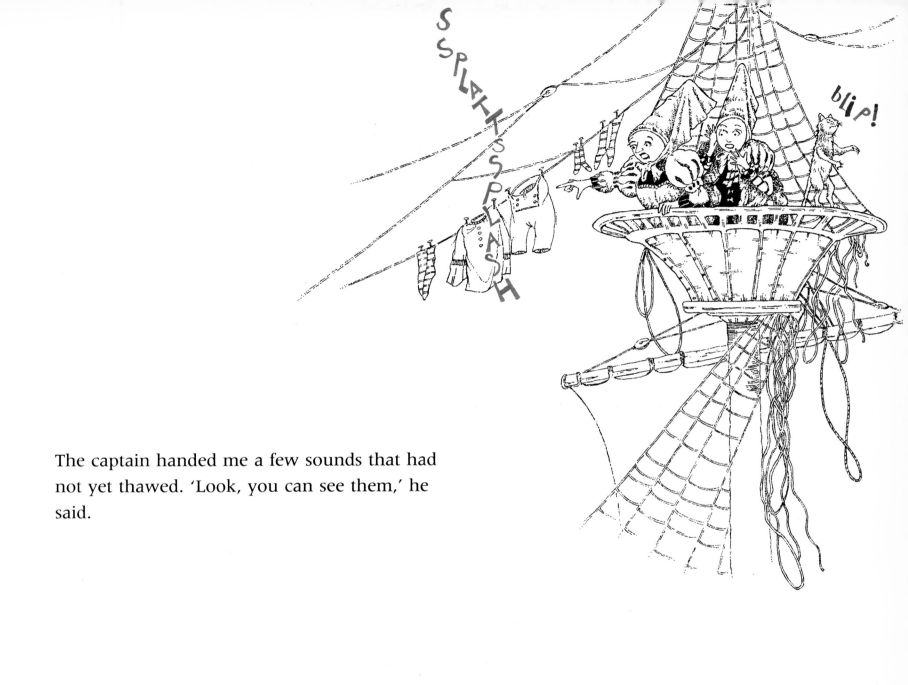

The captain handed me a few sounds that had not yet thawed. 'Look, you can see them,' he said.

We all grew quite merry then, and began snatching handfuls of the frozen sounds out of the air. We ran about shouting and laughing as we threw them onto the deck.

The children were catching at the brightly coloured ones and trying to eat them. Some of the sounds really did look like candy.

But whenever we tried to warm the frozen
sounds in our hands, they melted away like
snow.

And as they melted, they made strange noises:
some began to pipe and roll like fifes and drums,
while others pealed and blared like trumpets and
horns.

RATTLE PLONK SLAM CLASH PLUMP PLUMP FIZZLE SIZZLE SPLUTTER

The bosun found a very big frozen sound. While he held it in his hands it melted, giving out a rolling, thunderous boom that knocked him right off his feet.

'That was a cannon-shot,' said the captain.

BOOM

RATTLE

CREAK CREAK

SMACK SPLAT! PLOP!

THUD!

CRUNCH!

It was not only the big frozen sounds which needed to be handled carefully — some of the smaller ones were dangerous too.

'Ouch!' cried the cook's-boy. 'I just cut myself on a sharp word!'

Many of the words and sounds were terrible to look at.

Others were coarse and rude, and we blocked our ears against them.

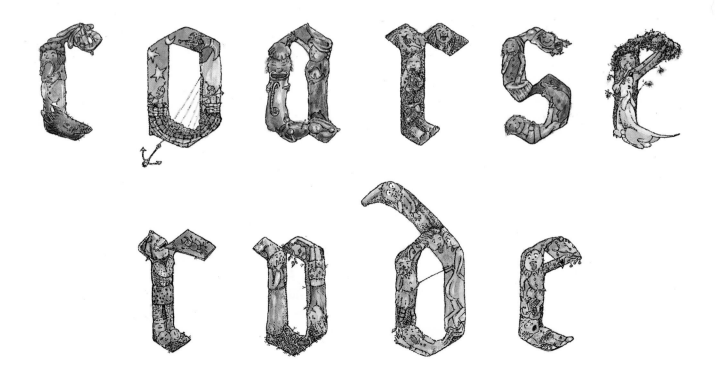

Others still were sharp, bleak and ugly.

sharp

bleak

ugly

In the end, we gathered up whole armfuls of the frozen sounds and threw them into a big heap, where they ran together and melted, making a very strange sizzling noise as they did so.

Then — BANG! WHOOSH! — they suddenly shot up into the sky like an enormous fireworks display.

clappaclappaclappaclappa

BOOOM

RUFF!

POKPOK!

PPPBUTTABUTTASPLUTTTERRSLUTTTERRSFiZZLE PiNG PoPPPoPPPPPPPPPPPPPPPPPPPP

TOKTOK

BONGGGGGGGG!!!

PLINK

QBOiiNNGgZiiNNGTOiiiNG!!!

ZZZZZOOOMMMOOOZZZAA

GLOBGLOP!!

CRUNCH

SCREEKK!

WHAM!

BONKk!

KERRPLONKK

SWOOOOSSHHHHHHHHH!!!!!

BANG

PEACE

At last, when all the frozen sounds had exploded and trailed away, the air became quiet again.

'Full speed ahead!' ordered the captain, and we sailed on our way, with nothing but a clear blue sky above us.

For Holly

With gratitude to Jeff Prentice
       who kept me on the right course
and François Rabelais
       who inspired me

Library of Congress Cataloging-in-Publication Data:

Walsh, Amanda.
    The mysterious hubbub / Amanda Walsh. — 1st American ed.
        p.   cm.
    Summary: A sailing-ship comes across the edge of the Frozen Sea,
    where a fierce battle had once been fought, and its screams and
    sounds which had been frozen in the cold air begin to melt.
    ISBN 0-395-53783-5
    [1. Sound—Fiction.] I. Title.
PZ7.W1665My 1990
[E]—dc20   89-26700
                                                 CIP
                                                 AC

Printed in Australia

10 9 8 7 6 5 4 3 2 1